TREASURE
FOR
LUNCH

by Shenaaz Nanji

Illustrated by Yvonne Cathcart

SECOND STORY Press

"I'm a sailor, and this is my ship," I sang, pulling my toboggan along over the snow. The sun shone as I headed for school. The ground was white, the trees were white, and the houses were white.

The warmth of my lunch bag made me take a peek. Golden potato fritters smiled at me. *Bhajias*! I shoved the bag into the darkness of my jacket pocket. Mom was out of town, so Grandma had made my lunch. I loved *bhajias*, but I was afraid to eat them in front of my friends. I was sure none of them had ever seen *bhajias* before.

Brring! When the school bell rang for lunch, a bell rang in my heart too. In the lunchroom, as lunch bags and lunch boxes opened, a rainbow of smells arose.

"Trade you a dino'wich!" Jessie held up her peanut-jelly sandwich, edges cut like the fangs of a dinosaur.

"Sure," Andy said. "I'll trade you my cheese sandwich."

"What do you have, Shaira?" Michael asked.

Ka-bam, ka-boom! My heart bounced in my chest like a soccer ball.

"I need to go to the bathroom," I said. But when I left the lunchroom, I headed straight out the front door.

Outside, my boots crunched the powdery carpet of snow. I trudged up the hill. A fierce wind howled across the schoolyard, a sound like the roaring waves of a white sea. Snowcapped stones lay scattered about the ground like seashells, and the snowy shrubs became seaweed. And here, at the top of the hill where I'd left it, was my toboggan, my ship.

I boarded my ship and pushed off hard with both hands. Skidoom! Down the hill I sailed. Cold winds whipped my face, flaring the sides of my unzipped jacket into twin red sails. Clouds of breath swirled in the air above me. My ship tipped over. Ahoy! I landed on Treasure Island!

I sat on my ship and gobbled my lunch. *Bhajias!* So many I couldn't finish. I dug a hole in the snow for what was left. "I'm a pirate burying treasure," I sang to myself. "This lunch will tell no tales."

Then I anchored my ship and raced back to find my friends.

Splat! Something cold and wet hit my neck.

"I've been looking for you," said Michael, his arms swimming through soft snow.

I scooped seas of snow and flung it at him until he was white as a ghost. Everyone laughed. My absence was forgotten. My secret was safe!

Next day, I waved goodbye to Grandma and towed my ship to school. The snow was deeper and whiter and softer than yesterday.

At lunch time, I dared to peek in my bag. Round brown meatballs peered up at me. *Kababs*! My mouth watered.

Ka-bam, ka-boom! My heart bounced in my chest.

"I need to call home," I told Jessie, and sneaked out to the playground before curious Michael arrived.

What a day! Millions of falling snowflakes twinkled like stars as I boarded my ship. I sailed to Treasure Island and gobbled my lunch. *Kababs!* So many I couldn't finish. I dug a hole in the snow for what was left.

"I'm a pirate burying treasure," I sang to myself. "This lunch will tell no tales."

Then I anchored my ship and raced back to find my friends.

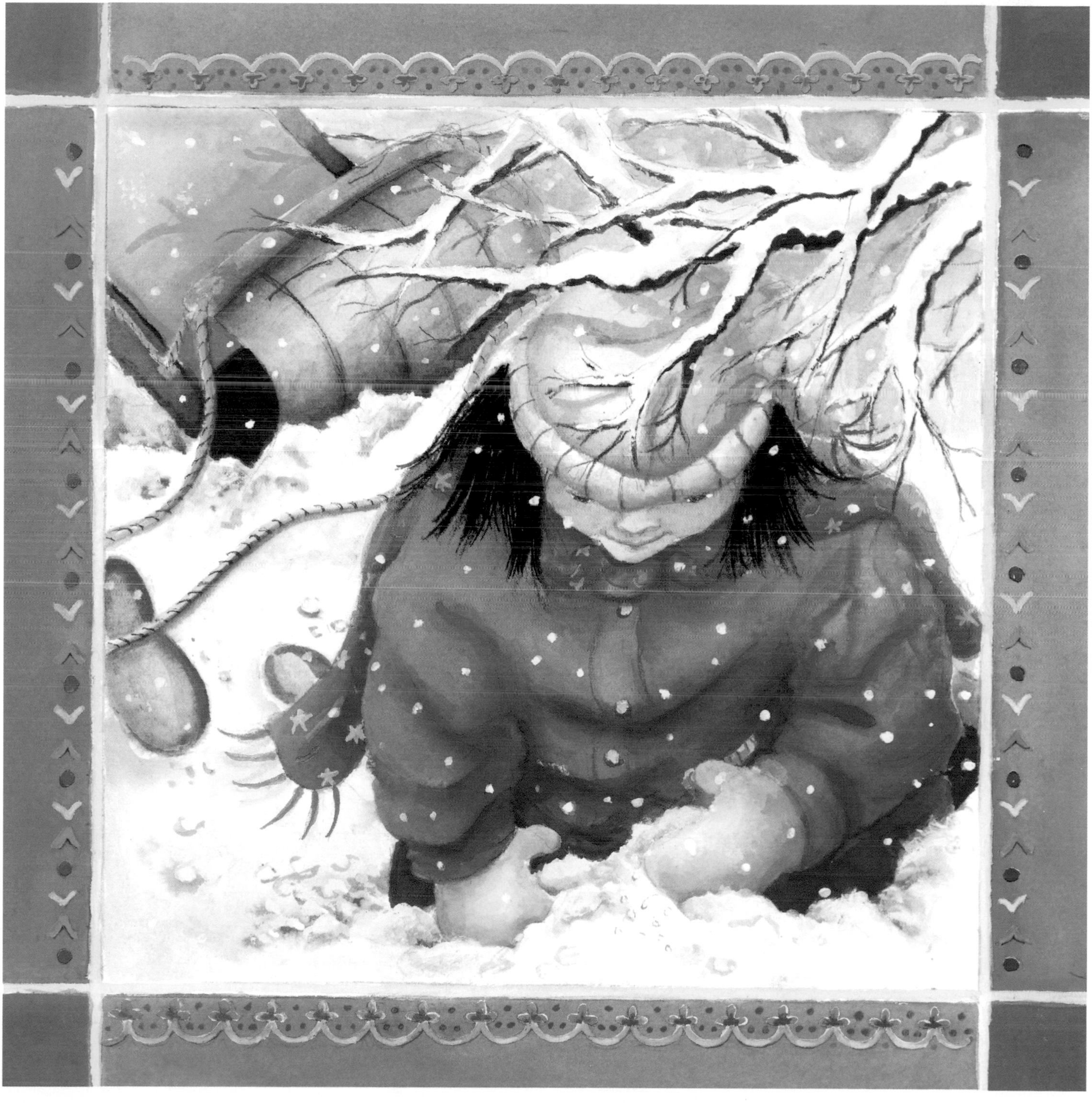

"I've been looking for you," Michael said, eyeing me suspiciously. "Where were you?"

"Want to make a snow tower?" I asked, trying to distract him.

"The tallest in the universe!" he cried.

We mounded and packed, scraped and shaped armloads of snow, and soon we had built a tower. Tiny ice crystals sparkled and glittered like diamonds in the sun.

"Tower of Diamonds!" I shouted. Everyone cheered, and we high-fived each other. My secret was still safe.

Next day, I left my ship at home. Warm winds of the Chinook were blowing, melting the snow into sloppy puddles. The great Chinook arch separated a clear blue sky from bleak purple clouds.

At lunchtime everyone rushed to eat outside. The playground was a checkerboard of puddles and dead grass. Our Tower of Diamonds had melted. I glanced down the hill. What was that peeping out of the slush like brown eyes?

Today Grandma had packed *samoosas* for lunch. My favourite! But how could I eat them in front of a sea of swimming eyes?

I ran to Michael. "Want to build another tower, buddy?" I pulled him to his feet.

"Yeah! Yeah!" Everyone shouted and ran after Michael to hunt for snow left under the trees. The coast was clear. Quickly I gobbled a *samoosa*.

Suddenly a voice rang out, "Treasure! I found treasure!"

I ran to my friends. And there, at the bottom of the hill, stood Michael, with everyone crowded around him.

"Look what I found," he said, lifting a soggy lunch bag from the ground. Through a tear in the bag my *kababs* looked like brown golf balls.

"Yours?" he asked Andy.

"Yours?" he asked Jessie.

"Yours?" he looked at me and added, "you always disappear at lunch."

All eyes were on me. I tried to shake my head. It stayed fixed like a rock.

"What's your secret lunch today?" Michael asked.

With trembling fingers I pulled out a crispy brown triangular pastry filled with spicy vegetable stuffing from my lunch bag. I offered it to Michael.

He took a bite.

"Delicious!"

A jungle of palms stretched towards me.

"Trade you my chocolate chip cookies?"

"Trade you my chips?"

"What're they called?" asked Jessica.

"*Samoosas,*" I said.

"*Samoosas*," echoed the others. "Can you bring some more tomorrow?"

"Sure!" I said.

"I'll ask Grandma to make *bhajias* and *kababs* too!"

To my children, Hussein and Shaira, and my husband.
— S.N.

To Zafar Shaikh for enriching my life with a culture different from my own.
— Y. C.

CHINOOK: A warm wind from the Pacific Ocean that blows over the Rocky Mountains into Alberta and sometimes Saskatchewan, causing a dramatic temperature rise in winter. An archlike cloud often accompanies the wind. Chinook means "snow eater" in the Chinookan Native language.

CANADIAN CATALOGUING IN PUBLICATION DATA

Nanji, Shenaaz
Treasure for lunch

ISBN 1-896764-32-0 (bound)

I. Cathcart, Yvonne. II. Title

PS8577.A573T73 2000   jC813'.54   C00-931103-3
PZ7.N36Tr 2000

Edited by Elise Levine
Printed in Hong Kong

Second Story Press gratefully acknowledges the assistance of the Ontario Arts Council and the Canada Council for the Arts for our publishing program. We acknowledge the financial support of the Government of Canada through the Book Publishing Industry Development Program (BPIDP) for our publishing activities.

Published by
SECOND STORY PRESS
*720 Bathurst Street, Suite 301
Toronto, Canada
M5S 2R4*